Dec. 2004

Janet,

   Thank you for all your supportive enthusiasm for poetry, and for your dedicated, careful proofreading.

Brian

ESSENTIAL POETS SERIES 127

**Canada Council
for the Arts**

**Conseil des Arts
du Canada**

ONTARIO ARTS COUNCIL
CONSEIL DES ARTS DE L'ONTARIO

Guernica Editions Inc. acknowledges the support of The Canada Council for the Arts.
Guernica Editions Inc. acknowledges the support of the Ontario Arts Council.

BRIAN DAY

AZURE

GUERNICA

TORONTO · BUFFALO · CHICAGO · LANCASTER (U.K.)

2004

Antonio D'Alfonso, editor
Guernica Editions Inc.
P.O. Box 117, Station P, Toronto (ON), Canada M5S 2S6
2250 Military Road, Tonawanda, N.Y. 14150-6000 U.S.A.

Distributors:
University of Toronto Press Distribution,
5201 Dufferin Street, Toronto, (ON), Canada M3H 5T8

Gazelle Book Services, White Cross Mills, High Town,
Lancaster LA1 1XS U.K.

Independent Publishers Group,
814 N. Franklin Street, Chicago, Il. 60610 U.S.A.

First edition.
Printed in Canada.

Legal Deposit – First Quarter
National Library of Canada
Library of Congress Catalog Card Number: 2003113947

National Library of Canada Cataloguing in Publication
Day, Brian
Azure / Brian Day.
(Essential poets series ; 127)
Poems.
ISBN 1-55071-190-3
I. Title. II. Series.
PS8557.A916A98 2004   C811'.6   C2003-906044-6

Contents

Preface

Many of the poems in this book are based on stories from South Asia, and particularly from the Hindu tradition. A little background information may be helpful in providing some context.

Several of the poems recount the various adventures of Vishnu, who is (with Brahma and Shiva) one of the three major gods of Hinduism, and who is often regarded primarily as the preserver or sustainer of the world. At times when life on Earth is threatened, he takes on an animal or human form (or avatar) and enters the world in order to save it. A number of the poems in this book deal with two of Vishnu's human avatars, Rama and Krishna.

The story of Rama is told in the Hindu epic *The Ramayana* (Rama's Journey). While the Ramayana deals extensively with battles and various other matters, I have focused in the poem sequence "Rama and Sita" on the relationship between Rama and his wife Sita. The story of their love is traditionally told in a manner in which Rama's actions are exemplary. His rejection and banishment of his wife are justified, and Sita docilely returns to him, patient and forgiving. I found this version difficult to accept and so have, while maintaining the major events of their story, considerably revised the motivations and characters of Rama and Sita.

Krishna, like Rama, is traditionally portrayed with blue skin. He is, particularly in his young adulthood, presented as a figure of amorous sensuality. He is often shown playing a flute, which embodies his fluid musical eroticism and draws his devotees toward him. Although both Rama and Krishna are regarded as avatars of Vishnu, each is distinct in personality. While Rama is often seen as an exemplar of duty and discipline, Krishna is more a figure of eroticism and play.

Some of the poems in this book may be made clearer by specific notes which will be found at the end of the volume.

Masks

Musée des Arts d'Afrique et d'Océanie, Paris

Here the first fur is scraped from my skull,
knots of rough grass plant the height of my forehead,
and spikes are driven, hard blessing, into bone.

Wisdom is splintered to the braiding of a brow,
lips are stitched like a purse of the gods,
and fear is taught the harsh punctures of joy.

In the strenuous grafting of death to smooth hide,
the face's fruit is carefully skinned.
The brain is left gagging and nearly still.

Raised to unbearable temperatures of beauty,
faces praise and beg for their own annihilation,
their eyes slit open and blazing with awe.

They have stalked through fields where flowers are on fire,
been scorched by the skin of animals' dreams,
held the memory like coals in the soft of their mouths.

They call me to drink from the bowl of their cheeks,
from wood as hard and polished as water.
From within the mask that I've become,

they're unflinchingly carving the bones of my skull,
gouging till my face is broken, adoring,
and I bear the markings where death is made whole.

Dark One

You are the smoothness of violets at dusk,
    the ache of berries for the deepening dark,
the muscle and pull of night's urgent river

drawing my eyes to delicious black drowning.
    A black rose of Sharon is my love among men,
as delicate as eyelids the dark petals of his skin.

You are the dark one bestowing black brilliance,
    whose beauty soaks light from the praise of my mouth.
You are oranges eaten sweet in the forest of the night.

You are black like the scent of ripening grapes,
    as dark as night's streams unsilvered by moonlight
and hymns that glisten with the flash of your flute.

As sweet as dark grapes on the press of my tongue
    is the face of my lord in the hour before morning.
His poetry pours like black orchids from my mouth.

Water-Lilies

Musée de l'Orangerie, Paris

In this egg room beneath the bright brooding city,
    at the feast of water's long marriage to light,
      art becomes altar that brims the eyes,
a curve where I enter and float without edges;
    where oil has been turned to water and wine
      and eyes drink delicious cool glasses of light.
Streamed with wet fronds and ribbons of colour
    I would glide immersed to the end of my days
      in this watery solemnity of petals and stems
where a tendering green forms the borders of blue,
    paint divines the true colour of water,
      and cool slips of the fecund are brushed on my eyes.
The hopes of my face are replenished by water,
    the colours of art drench deep in my skin,
      and the weight of the world is mere flowers in my arms.

Palace of Glass

Across the near and uncrossable water
   glints the intricate palace of glass
where my love lies still in the first light of morning.
   I wake to his beauty as he wakes on his bed,
a single bird turning in time's frozen tree.
   I watch in near worship the shape of his rising,
his branching extension of hands to the sky.
   He splashes his face and hair with cool water
that briefly glasses the beauty of his features,
   beads on his lashes, steals a trickle down his chest.
He lowers himself to the mat of his prayers,
   holds himself still as a bird beneath eyelids,
composing himself to the fine scent of praise.
   From a chest of red and inlaid wood
he lifts sheaf of paper, smoothed tools of writing,
   sits at a table by windowing walls
and gives like a smooth unobstructed vein
   the stream of his life to the pages beneath him.
I glimpse in his lines the glass of my words,
   and the fingers of my mind move smoothly in his.
Could I but cross that uncrossable water
   I would seek him in that glinting of diamond and pane.
We would be two men wed on one side of the mirror.
   We would love with our bodies clothed with glass.

Campus

He was a young man I might have paid for:
    not for rumple of bedsheets in a nearby room,
but merely for the private demonstration of his beauty.
    My eyes like a tiger would lick his torso,
and the flicking of his smile over triceps and lips
    would convert me to the work and the postures of devotion.
I'd offer him sea-green pictures of my queen,
    the first and Anglican defender of my faith.
Taught that God could enter the body of a man,
    I'm alert to the neglected stages of epiphany
that bring longing for flesh and a perfecter world.
    As he skins the white T-shirt obscuring the holy,
the meter of my heart in seconds is wound tight,
    and I'm charmed seeing spirit to such muscle poured.
He recalls my lulled and purblind eyes
    to a radiance blazing beneath the mundane.
He prisms clean light into myriad forms,
    reminds me of the lovely in the plain field of faces.
Beyond the aureole of his lights and music,
    money's spent without glamour to buy sandwiches and pop
for those poorly clad and less perfect of skin
    who shiver against the night's buffets of cold.
He has scattered a mist of delectable light
    scented with incense, sweat, and beneficence.

Jardin du Luxembourg

Saturday afternoon, boats sail
on the fountain.
A man sitting on the wall holds bread
in his hands
where birds impeccably land to eat –
was St. Francis
ever so beautiful? A woman, feet resting
on a chair,
reads from a book jacketed in white,
a boy strikes
at a nut tree with a newspaper tube,
runners stained
with shapes of sweat stride by,
and a young couple,
walking, stops to kiss. Everywhere are men –
like him, reclined,
face turned to the sun, too beautiful
not to hold
some knowledge surpassing my own. From
behind a statue
the sun slants to my eyes, leaves me swelling and
empty with joy.

Paris of Days

In these, the most Paris of days,
    thirst trickles clear and delicious
in my veins as I bare to Paris
    the skin of all my incipient
senses and the world sips smoothly
    from the vial of my bones.

Heavens are cradled in the city's
    rose fingers and we are frail
matches in this city of light
    where my every nerve is in prayer
with Paris and the kingdom
    of senses is surely among us.

Flesh of My Flesh

As I melt to the senses of sleep
they are roused, emerge
from the crimson and silver
of veils, embrace in the incense-thick
fog of my flesh. Brushing their smiles
on the lips of my eyes,
they smooth me with oils and aroma
of clove, trace their trained fingers
over moistness and mind. They taste
smooth gooseberry brimmings of flesh,
their love a tear gland
in the eye of my dream.
They cavort in the forest
of my toes' phalanges, scamper
with their secrets between muscles'
sheets, stretching in my limbs
limbs schooled in love, and mapping
with their tongues
the nerves' tightropes of pleasure.

I wake with my flesh all revived
by their love, each pillar
and cornice of my polished bones,
each muscle and fascia licked
lovely as milk. Swept clean
as a brothel and parlour
of love, I rise as the temple
quickened by their senses, the gifts
of their coupling still
glistening on my skin.

Praying in Sport

I summon you with drumming from beneath my ribs,
invoke you with quick urgent intakes of air.

You are no stillness but blood-beating speed –
a holiness restless, elastic, athletic.

As I climb the spiralling stairways of bone,
pink air pressed out from the canyons of my chest,

you are the player quick-plucking my blood,
hounding my body as the hunter's own prey.

My lungs have laced themselves drunk with air
and blaze with neon in each of their filaments.

You are beaded like morning dew on my arms,
a god who glistens in this vestment of sweat –

who drips on the parchment prayerbooks of my skull
and cleans the fish-slick fissures of my brain.

You're my ecstatic, my lane-mate, my team,
driving my heart to its ceiling of speed –

and we race through the brilliant minutes of exertion
in prayer a white thunder, a fluorescence of flesh.

In Others' Skin

Having known the cool pink pill of athletics
to bolster the sexual wattage of my cells
and sweeten by teaspoons the raw sugar in my blood,

I crave other creatures shaped by exertion,
whose bodies are crafted by disciplined practice,
engorged in each of their packets of pleasure.

Strolling the rows in carnality's orchards,
I've reached for men carved hard with work,
polished their strenuous, constructed shapes,

tasted them as fruit might taste its own flesh,
pressed my limbs beneath each of their weights,
known my pores beaded with the sweat of their effort.

I've boasted their bodies, delicious as marble,
been lit by their nerves and wires of gold,
felt their power like quicksilver licking my veins.

I've glowed with rewards of their hard repetitions.
And the labour of training that peaked in their cries
is laid as bright ore in the records of my flesh.

Dancing Priests

The first gay bar I went to was littered
with priests, each cradling a glass of sweet
golden liquid and offering, on his trips

to the bar, a drink. When that month's anthem
pounded through the speakers, they processed
en masse to the slick of the dancefloor,

where abandoning all their collars'
constraints, they lifted their hands
in a new consecration and cast

out nets to fish for men, here
where celibacy knew no bounds
and the commandments of their days

were suspended by night. And I
was entranced by the subtle magic
that allowed them to dance in these storeyed

worlds, their lives like chasubles
sleekly reversed, each face
satin and unblemished in its skin.

Priest at the Altar

Infatuated with the Catholic and considering the cloth, I met
A priest of the kind I wanted to be: vibrant, undeceived,
Independent in thought. Only recently received
To the Church, I was seeking a vocation – but not quite yet,
Not until I'd sampled other offerings of love.
He invited me to take an afternoon walk. He invited
Me for drinks, to an opera. He eyed me and discreetly waited
Until I voiced our attraction. He did not rebuff
Me, assured me his celibacy would not be stained,
Elicited from me a vow of silence. Illicit
Privilege assured my compliance. And I slept in a delicious
Conjoining of desires: sex was no longer simply profane.
The next morning at mass there was nothing to be sacrificed:
The man who'd drunk deeply from the cup of my skin
Placed bread in the cup of my hands, half-grinned,
And addressed me at the altar: the Body of Christ.

The Centre Cannot Hold

The centre cannot hold its breath any longer.
  It's not that some conquering order returns
But that all this moment's frictional bearings
  Assemble to a nuclear aggregate of stars,
A gravity greater than any we've circled.
  We sense that this floating turtle's back
Holds shapes beyond the one we're boxed in,
  Expands in the patterns of an adult geometry,
Still forms the eye of the ocean's orbit.
  The figures and courses of the divine are multiplied:
A smooth round pan, a bowl of silver
  Where marbles circle, form ellipses and systems,
Trace and inscribe a cursive whole.
  We've misunderstood the being whose feet
Would slip through the mental membrane of the sky:
  As if heaven could be a one-man show,
Not a team of prime donne mobiles.
  The merest of anarchies binds them together –
As in that cone where eagles are born
  And fractured branches are compiled to a home.
A shred of beauty is delivered to our throats,
  A scrap of scripture, and there rises the sand
That smooths the border between eyes and brain.
  Lines have been slit in the sky like an iris.
Bending knees in devotion to this new dispensation,
  We step up to the stage of divine promiscuity.

Mount Athos

After the reliquary's treasures have been shown – the leprous
left hand of Mary Magdalene and diversely
brown fragments of the one true cross – a monk
leads me from the chapel to the westerly balcony, where
    before us
lie all the kingdoms of Europe; and he asks me
to brief him on the state of my faith. I describe a loose
and inchoate federation, a league of old stories and jostling
beliefs. He frowns at my slovenly habits of spirit,
asks why one good church does not suffice. Pages
of my mind have been starkly illumined
by the stars of far unfamiliar
religions, and I can't presume foreign sages
do not pulse in God's wrists.
He warns me of the dangers of the Hindu
east, of transplanting a soul in foreign soil, of the great
perdition that lurks in the plural. I have bitten
polished skin which he would call heresy, found God smiling
    slyly
in forbidden flavours, and I know
there's no completion to the books
of revelation, no seal
to silence the profusion of prophets. "It's your soul,"
he says when the sun has been swallowed and he
gives me up to the sky's wild stars. He returns
to his cell to work out his salvation, and for minutes
I envy his possession of a map; then pray
to live always in danger of amazement. I ask this
of a God I cannot imagine – who speaks in a whirling
    pandemonium
of tongues and sits with quiet multiplied
faces three steps beyond the lips of this world.

The Creation of the Goddess

The gods themselves are in need of new deity. Butting
its head on the blue gates of heaven
a demon is drooling in its rage
for upheaval. With buffalo horns it's torn
peace from the Earth, gorgoned its fields
to desert and stone, riddled
the oceans and sky with effluents. The gods
have been driven to the edge of extinction, need
a power that surpasses their own. They play
their hands in creation's ante: each
shoots his energy, spirit-form
of muscle, into the smooth-rimmed cauldron
of the sky, whitening the heavens
with ejaculate light. There from the urgent
offering of the gods blazes a scalding
profusion of divinity, a Fury-tongued
warrior and compaction of faith. She assaults
like a tide crash on the inner ear, is coloured
bright as comics to protect
the planet. Edged with the sky's
own azaleas of light, she makes her birth loud
as a law and irrevocable, a swift queenly
coup in a palace of bones. She tears
like an animal's tonsils and tongue the demon's
hot life from the purse of its skin. Carrying
the savage blue beads
of creation, she advances in a
deluge of pelting lights, sutures the thinning
frayed skin of the world. Not held
in the reigns of her many creators, she concocts
her masala from their fine
contributions, collects like spilled thunder the force

of old gods. Exacting as a cook
or a cool executioner, she assembles
the thick winter soup
of her love, presses shreds
of sharp death into dishes of wonder, drips
her raw danger like sauce on our skin.

Alligator Pie

After Dennis Lee

At the theatre a poster for *Alligator Pie*,
and earlier that day at the zoo I'd read
of elephant steaks being sold in the supermarket,
of ministry officials feasting on gorilla.

We flake like pastry the skin of our Goddess,
savour the taste of each of her features,
excise her vocal chords, feast on rare birds,
consume what no future generation will hear.

We slice open lives we no longer speak to,
push to our mouths the whole host of animals;
but the tickling cosmos is caught in our throats
and their loping spirits cannot enter our blood.

A friend of mine has donated his organs
to any mammal who needs them to live:
returning to creatures who no longer eat us
the taste and the liquor of human cells.

Weighing this now, a vestigial Christian,
I would offer my flesh to be eaten by animals.
To their need I would give my full human folly,
my body as useful as any day's eucharist.

Byzantine Museum, Corfu

In the gilt-lit air of this religion, the sky
is flaked with gold. Stepping in from the fair ocean
light outside, I'm slow to perceive the distortions
here: these perspectiveless panels where proportions
are jack-knifed, each story's employed as devotion's
needle, and I'm accosted by the vigilant eyes

of saints and multiplied, unified gods. The first
is the knightly crusader, St. George; and seated
behind him as a wooden fairy, a prim and elf-
like warrior, is the steady homunculus clone of himself:
his body and armour all minutely repeated
but with the apprehension of the larger reversed

to the calm assurance of victory. Next, almost Hindu
in the doubling of his extended hands, St. Panteleemon
accuses me of being milksop mild, average
in my watered half-humanity, not baked and savaged
by the glare and prods of God and demons,
the fires that leave the brain blistered and new.

Be a saint and surely you'll come to great harm.
John, fed on the buzz and crack of locusts,
was as tolerant as thorn, arraigned and attacked
by curvaceous, voluptuous dancing. He stands intact,
the harsh maleness of his eyes now focused
on mine, his severed head held bleeding in his arms.

The hardest, least forgiving of the faces is Christ.
As stern as a patriarch, he dares me to any
unorthodox thought, scours any filth that may cling
to my beliefs, bleaching and remaking
the plot of my brain, fixing me for when he
will douse all the joy that the flesh delights

in. Finally, Christ sits for his family portrait.
The old man floats remote in his heaven. Both frown,
sworn enemies of time, and grow older. But there, blurred
in the white shock of movement between them, is a bird
escaping from the men of God, surging in feathered impulse
    down
to break through the gilt of the picture's border.

Extinguishing the Animals

He brought them to the man to see what he would call them, and whatever the man called each living creature, that was its name.

Genesis 2.19

Adam each hour is forgetting names,
drawers of his mind drawing thick with darkness.
He is counting backwards the days of creation,
returning to a world not cushioned against him,
where grass is not nibbled beneath his feet,
all kinds and colours of animals are collapsed
into rock and water, light and dark:
encasing the world in the egg of its chaos.

He holds a bright history of wavering candles,
considers his limitless list of wishes.

He's unlearning the sound of each animal's voice,
scraping their cadences from the raw of his throat.
He's surrendering the shapes of all his familiars:
the thick of a presence that beat in his blood,
the birds that have lit the thoughts of God.
He shuts the one case of original icons,
will feel no fresh imprint of feet in his brain.

All creatures are compressed from flesh to idea.
Reducing so much of the world to mere spirit,
he's condemned to live less in the land of his body,
begins the migration outside of his skin.

Adam presides at the funeral of animals,
raises to his lips a communal cup
where a dark wine, shivering, pales to water,
then, with a breath from his mouth, goes out.
His prayers thin briefly till he cannot speak,
and no one will walk in the garden at evening.
The man has finally spoken their names
and dispenses their memory to the sweeping wind.

Blue Jesus

You are blue as twilight
   in the garden of Eden,
blue as night's footsteps
   by the river Yamuna.
You wade through the dreams
   of our waiting world,
step up to the black
   and skittering surface,
tread a thin mirror
   over maundering fish,
reach your long fingers
   round the colours of the globe.

The dark of Gethsemane
   shines in your eyes,
your hands are licked
   by the deep water serpent,
and there's no one behind you
   but a vault without a voice.
You know sure as azure
   where night will lead you.
The sky will be torn
   like a bolt of blue fabric
and we'll stand in that
   silent snow of threads.

The Love Between Krishna and Jesus

They approach one another with cool flowers of language,
move their mouths in the gorgeous recitation of beauty;

speak with the unpenned poetry of scripture,
the memory behind words of the blue walks of heaven.

After rage at armies and amassers of money,
each shows the other his friendly form,

withdraws from the gaping ground of his battles
to the secluded pool of nakedness and bathing;

eases to a heart as capacious as his own,
awakes the faint world with fresh adoration.

Hands trace over skin as sure sacred text,
ponder as patiently, savour as deep.

These princes of devotion, co-creators of love,
make themselves love on the plane of their skin,

blurring their words to a once-fused language,
their forms to one sinuous glistening of delight.

They meld themselves to this moist skin and strength,
retuning their limbs to the bright keys of heaven:

agape that these bodies bred from stars
could harbour such awe at the pouring of pleasure:

at skin newly lit and expansive as sky,
at the quick touch of wonder in a night of such eyes.

Krishna has blossomed as the season of flowers
and Jesus the fig tree now heavy with bloom.

They meet as the alpha and snake tail of time,
the clasp that unites bright intimate worlds.

Radha

I long for the long blue body
    of Krishna: to feel his dark eyes
fill me with light, to know his gaze
    grazing over my skin. This
would be the blessing of princes
    upon me. This would be
the flower of heaven on my tongue.

I watch the smooth blue
    body of Krishna, draped and snaking
on a strong low bough. He
    in his mischief has stolen our clothing
and we stand naked before him
    in water. Only Krishna can clothe us
in perfect light, only he can see our skin
    without shame and offer us clothing
that leaves us uncovered, the play
    of our skin still grinning in his eyes.

As smooth as butter
                            is Krishna's mouth,
as full of pleasure
                            as the rounded heavens:
his body as blue
                            as the last light of evening,
as the darkness that gives
                            to the mysteries of love.

I long for the garlanded door
   of his flesh, for the scent
of his neck, his lithe clear limbs;
   for his burnished body,
the bright garment of god.
   I want with my blood to dance
with lord Krishna, to turn with his eyes
   fixed forever on mine,
to be taken in the great
   blue cloud of his love.

With Krishna I would know

                 the fragrance of the world.
I would be in each moment

                 polished by his beauty.
I would glow forever

             with a lustre of blue.

Mourning Krishna

Like the udders of cows we have withered and dried;
    our figures have slackened in the absence of Krishna,
and the gloss of desire is robbed from our days.
    The Yamuna flows torpid and slow as our hours;
the air stands motionless, musicless, dead.
    Krishna's mischief as a monkey does not leap among trees
or trick the village with the laughter of his pranks,
    and no one undresses our thoughts with his flute,
moves his feet in the measure of our pattering pulse.
    We are parched for the briefest glimpse of his presence:
as he slips by us to steal our sweet butter,
    marked in our minds by his smear of blue.

The beating of drums calls our feet to the forest
    as his flute once enticed us to his feet in the grove,
and there before us stand the glories of Krishna,
    his body repeated, bright columns in darkness.
Our breasts crave to be held like the world in his palms,
    to be licked with an infant's absolute hunger,
a cerulean flutist's infinite skill.
    I race to the stately slim figure of Krishna,
place my hands on the slender calm strength of his hips,
    press my length to the smooth curved pillar of his skin.
And his eyes are empty, a statue's wood.
    At each tree is repeated the pitiful sight
of my sister embracing the smoothness of bark,
    caressing the skin she would stroke into Krishna.
They each hold their lover for a thick melting moment
    before they admit the cold waters of grief,
see the body of Krishna has left them twice widowed,
    his flesh and his music again robbed from their skin.
Krishna has left us no more than his trees,

35

and each of us tenderly returns to its comforts,
tending its body as the limbs of our lord,
    held by dark trees in our Krishna's own arms.

Krishna at the Mirror

Krishna stands poised in the face of the mirror,
extends his arm in a curve of greeting
that invites and is met by the partner before him,
and Krishna dances deftly with the world in himself.

It's a bright boy who partners him now in the glass
and suggests the quick step that Krishna joins,
matching the man his impulse has made.
Turning in the tacit camaraderie of mirrors,

he perceives the form of a woman before him,
a dancer who angles her eyes to meet his
and calls him to still more liquid motion
as she pours her body like milk to his eyes.

And Krishna is enamoured of the figure in the glass,
the meeting and merging of maker and man,
a face nearly his, and like all the world, him.
He greets himself as a friend in the mirror,

smiles at the selves he slips into his skin,
his reflection returning to its accustomed form
as he meets eyes again that are wholly his own
and delights like a stranger in the grace of his limbs.

Shiva Nataraja

His dancing is balanced with one foot on ignorance
    that squirms beneath him like a scheming child.
    He holds in the high right hand of creation
the drum which beats the world into being

and assigns the rhythm to the current of his limbs.
    In his high left he holds the quick fire of destruction,
    ready to extinguish the great fiction of forms.
He's a twin in the oozing egg of creation,

a man and a woman fused in one skin,
    dances doubled in gender and extremity,
    construing religion from the motions of his flesh
and breathing his indifferent blessing on the world.

The swaying of his body like a lotus on its stem
    extracts the hard holiness from the minerals of the earth.
    Inscribed in the flaming circle of his dance, as steady
as a saint, he offers his body's slow stirring of light.

Here in the heat of annihilating glory
    a smile sits like stillness in the midst of copulation.
    He finger-drums the world to its purr of existence
and spreads the warm honey of death on our eyes.

Shiva and Jesus Drink Poison

When the milky sea is churned for its soma,
what rises first
to the surface is poison. Shiva sights this
as his first sweet chance
to become adored as a dangerous god. To protect
the whole body
of the infant world, he sips the bitter risen
cream. The liquid
pools in the chambers of his throat, staining
his larynx blue
with destruction. And the smoothness of his neck
is rich with lapis,
pulsing like the ocean, venom swollen
to a beating jewel.

Jesus in the garden reaches for the brimming
cup of his death,
invites the grace of the Judas kiss. He offers his
mouth as a rapturous
suicide, won't resist being taken. He is never
so radiant and glistening
in his skin as when he is subject to the soldier's
scourge, and vinegar
purples the old wine of his throat. Nearly stripped
and erotically muscled,
he hangs taut on the cross with sorrow and strength,
the plates of his torso
lifted up for adoration, and his face suffering all
the affliction of God.

We'd lick the powerful column of his neck,
the pillar stained with heaven's colours,
suck the blue stone of his voice's fruit.

We'd love to explore with the doubt of our fingers
the lovely inviting wound of his side
and trace the interior cathedrals of his flesh.

They've offered their lips to kiss
liquid evil, savoured its sharp mature taste
on their tongues. They have passed beyond
the fledgling pages of goodness, known
the thick ink of destruction tattooed
in their skin. Their bodies have both
been adorned with anguish, display
the bruised beauty of maleness broken.
They've surrendered their mouths for the band
of their cohorts, sipped sordid liquids
that would addle the brains of lesser men;
and poison hovers ready as love in their eyes.

Shiva Dances with Krishna

Shiva sits alone on the mountain,
his mind a black lake beneath the range.
It's music that awakens the deep stone
of his belly, lifts him with forgotten
gusts of desire, a thirst that's been buried
beneath meditation's weight. Music purls
over stones just beneath his skin, whets
this novel thirst in his limbs. On legs
with distant memories of dancing, he steps
through the moistened scents of the forest,
descends to be rinsed in the cool
of the river.
    On the far bank he emerges,
sheeting and wet with the warm drops
of need. Around him are a hundred pressing
women, each one winding her way toward
Krishna. Shiva shares their insatiable
thirst: for his eyes and ears to be stuffed
with this beauty, for the fabric of this music
to be stitched in his skin, and the threads of it
needled like stars through his nerves.
After labours alone in the chambers
of his heart, he sights joy's shape
in the blue flesh before him, and the taste is sweet
on the roots of his tongue.
    Krishna's clear flute
incites him to dance, and his eyes caress
the quick eyes of this youth, who has never enjoyed
so consummate a partner, a dancer
who fills the skin of each phrase, leading
the music as he follows its need,
and giving breath to the notes his body

performs. They dance as the wedding of men
in their art: Shiva the lithe profusion of desire,
and Krishna the brilliant fleet trilling of love.

Krishna Speaks from the Whirlwind

You offer the sweet scented smoke of your questions,
   confer as a human with the great vault of heaven.
As a tireless scholar you inquire of your God,
   and I entertain each of your queries with pleasure,
   invite your brave scaling of matter and mind.

You have lived from before the birth of black oceans,
   from before the sky's darkness was chipped into days.
You were the shimmering beneath quavers of music
   when the stars of morning began their chorus
   and raised their voices in rays of song.
I saw you and formed you as time cracked its first smile.

When the back of the land was arched into mountains
   and rock clothed itself in layers of light,
   you shifted as a glittering of crystals and colour,
   a vein of motion in an opus of stone.
When clouds were weighing their first thoughts of rain,
   you were even then beaded moist in my breath.
You know in your body the rhythm of waters,
   the green glass and lace and pummelling of tides.
And as Earth was choosing its cherished pigments,
   you decked yourself in abundance of green
   and umbrellaed the land in your hunger for light.

You have lived as enzymes in the lizard's green belly,
   slept with dark gall in the bladder of the bear,
   whispered air to the intricate bones of terns.
You apprenticed in the art of the crocodile's creation,
   inside his hard body crept coolly toward prey.
Together we entered the horse's swift flesh:
   its flanks that glistened with explosive muscle,
   its strength that trembles like the locust's wing.

When your mother strained like a planet in travail
    I wrapped you in the many-petalled wishes of your birth.
I have held you through each heartbreak of childhood and loss,
    directing the drama where you act with abandon
    through swells of great ungainsayable grief
    and flashes of joy brighter yellow than gold.

Inquire as deeply as your words can plumb;
    with your quiver of questions I am well pleased.
You are a man and a parcel of freedom,
    a woman and a nudging of the ceiling of sky.
Like a lover you pluck at the coverings of the world,
    and I revel in all creatures who pursue their gods,
    am lit by their prayers as a sky drenched with stars.
You glint in the spinning of entreaty and invention,
    refashion the world with your listening hands.
You inhabit one tree that is vision, creation,
    dart with allurement among flower and leaf,
    and when I see you flitting, it's from home to home.

Vishnu, Seductive

His hand passes as a mirror in front of his eyes,
    a tinkling of bangles invests the ear,
there's a softness like the cooling of air after rain,
    and the hip of heaven tilts on its axis.

The eternal takes on an hourglass figure,
    silk wraps the unwrappable feast of her skin,
and features are rewritten in a skilled brush of beauty,
    her throat grown enticingly smooth as laughter.

Her hair floats, a soft sheet of secrets around her,
    lips tremble with invitations more luscious than words,
and the flash of her eye is delight's bold invention,
    her perfume a ribbon that unbuckles men's brains.

She glides demurely through the congress of gods,
    wafting their eyes like moths on the air,
evoking the sighs and the pounding desire
    she will take as her credit but decline to redeem.

Sukanya and the Ant Man

My husband's the man I found in an anthill.
Abandoned by ambitious and thankless progeny
who needed him like the stink of old skin on their necks,
he spread, as a man will, into the ground,
his skin as inviting to ants as stale sugar.

Passing that animate pustule of land,
I was tracked by the burning of tiny bright eyes
as red as itching sharp scabs of light.
I poked them, with a stick, like you'd poke at a snake.

The next day the plague invaded our intestines:
no human in the land could budge their bowels.
For days we were clotted with our own weighty refuse,
swelling with the turgid dark mass of ourselves.

Such stasis can destroy the reign of a king.
My father was king, asked of any indiscretion
I might have committed in unknowing offence.
I'd poked a stick to an anthill's eyes.
It was as though I had peed in the temple of Shiva.

"An anthill's the delicate ear of the earth,
the timpani that measures the nemesis of heaven;
it's the trap door to the workings of the world," he said.
He hurried me to the mound. There arose a rustle
of dry leaves and laughter
                              and the anthill spoke:
"Two options," he said, like the flip of a leaf:
"You kill her or tomorrow she becomes my wife."
I was caught in the noose of a nation's bowels.

A day holds many hours when you don't touch your husband,
and even the ant-stink crawling on my skin
would surely be worth the birdsong and mangoes,
the cool walks of morning and still moments in shade.

The body I'd reserved for a sleek young lover
would be lowered to the dusty slack arms of this grave.
After threat of death I was marrying a disease
I would carry incurably in the itch of my skin.

On the day of my wedding I entered my mourning:
before bathing I peeled off the pleasures of my flesh,
and I scented my skin with a widow's aloes. The touch
of my wedding dress was numbing as a shroud,
its hems all embroidered like the trails of ants.

And he shuffled beside me to our mouldering bed.
His hands on my body brought waftings of warmth,
surprised me as a wholly misplaced season.
Gently as a grandfather's they fingered through my hair
with a care that made me sweet myrrh in his eyes.
My beauty was more treasured than ever it had been –
but my hands could not learn the desire to touch him,
his body a sack hung with random loose bones.

My days were a fever of supple young men
whose ventures brought slick and visual joy
to all the starved organs of my carnal sight.
My mind leapt acrobatic with inventions of sex,
couplings and triplings in intricate postures,
grand circus feats of finesse and exhaustion.
And my eyes were never so erotically drenched
as when I descended to the cool Sarasvati.

Once as I bathed I saw the world steal
a scene I had practised and polished in my mind:
two men who dripped with luscious young strength,
their skin smooth and licked as perfect meniscus.
Seeing dreams in flesh, I watched, confounded.

The world had opened a mirror of itself,
so perfect their symmetry down the centre of my sight:
one's left foot cocked to the other's right,
one's half-smile matched in the mouth of his twin.

They approached me like drunken and heavenly vision,
addressed the caressing dark words of my praise;
questioned how a woman so exquisite in her skin,
so glistening with the intimate urges of youth,
could be kept by a man who'd been barely scraped up
as he slid to decay in the larvae of his grave.

My body like a separate person approached them
to engage in their elaborate choreography of love.
And I stopped in cold hatred, water lapping at my ankles.
I wanted them angrily, like the crash of the sky.
I wanted them like the unbroken world I had lost.

I walk down the gauntlet and seam of their mirror,
my skin burned by skin I'm refusing to touch.
They weigh my distress in the weight of their bodies,
know I crave them like eyes on the sides of my head.

There's no one to flee to but my husband himself.
He hears with calm of the twins' apparition,
hears, I am sure, the slipping in my voice,
and I won't have the strength to refuse them again.

His words come slowly and without his surprise.
"You will have," he tells me, "both things you desire."
He holds in his age and terrestrial memory
the secret of the liquid the divine twins desire:
the soma that's guarded and sipped by the gods
and tastes of honey on the spirit's tongue.

He'll offer the secret – they will not say *no* –
and as payment we'll have my old husband transformed
to the tripling likeness of the limber twins,
his new skin as sleek as the shells of oysters,
and his limbs the accomplished young artists of love.

I know that I should be grateful, exultant,
cradling this gold plum my husband has crafted
by sealing its clearly unmatchable halves.
And a crevice of mourning cracks deep through my brain.

All of my worlds will be shattered into one.
I will be blessed with a killing contentment
and breed with the thoughts of a single man's skin.
I have traced the misted horsetails of beauty
that cavort on the horizon and meadows of the mind.
I have woken from a thousand simmering daydreams
with the attar and gloss of their flavours on my skin.
And after today I will not wake again.

Avatar

Who can remember his own
incarnation, the funnelling of heaven to a vessel
of flesh? Though his plans are stitched with invisible thread
to the cool grinning absence
of himself in the sky, he can find no pattern
to the pull of his days. When the fluids of his brain
have bittered to vinegar and his mouth
is an aviary of desert birds, his skin is licked
by vicarious flames and he suffers the ingress of steel between
    ribs.
Forsaken by the prayers of his fathers'
religion, by the last slipping cells
of his desperate brain, he stands bewildered in a fountain
of petals, white flowers confetti his marriage to heaven:
there's God thick as tarpaper under his skull.

He's aimed himself sharply at the grave's cold eye,
had extinction stolen like a bone
beneath his nose. In clothing still wet with the grey blood
of demons, he awakes on his easter to a dream
that won't end. Agape at his sleight at decoying death, he can't
yet concede that the magic is his, can't finger
the track to this spindling
existence, to these insect eyes that kaleidoscope the world.
He's a phoenix with feather gaps burned in his memory.

Dumb as a human in the school of heaven, he receives
gods descending from the theatre of their seats to whisper
discreetly the syllables of his name. It's proclaimed as a carnival
that today is his birthday, and the broad world holds nothing
outside of himself: it's lit
with the fevered colours of dreams that creep

like criminals down the alleys of his thoughts. He delights
like a paupered king in his return, sorting the borders
and passwords of the real, testing for madness all the leaks
of his skull. He's plunged toward what was certain drowning
and found himself blessed with amphibian lungs.
He lurches like a drunkard from humility to fraud.

It shadows his mind that he is now
no one, he sips on this coolness as his face
evaporates, and he knows it as purely as the green
of leaves. Here, in this harsh exponential adulthood, he knows
the most vicious voices are his own, that sages
and slanderers are all pitches of his throat, and he
is the arcing nib of their story. The eyes of a snake
are planted in his throat, and he slides
through the moist new air of history,
seduced by lotus, his own body's odour.

He craves the white peace of human sleep, the retiring
of a mind to passive inventions. He lays like a pouch
of diamonds beside him the knowledge that his
is the voice of creation, opens the door for his chosen
betrayer, thumbs the slim pack of his human memories.
He prays to each clenched corner of himself
to release him from the burden of being divine, the task
of endlessly speaking the world. He prays, his body
unrolls like fields, and there slips from his mouth like a raft of
    tears
the precious, forgettable voice of God.

Rama and Sita

I

The Birth of Rama

King Dasaratha desires a son. He craves the smile
of his own unlined face on the future, his own ink bright
in the kingdom's composition. A man advanced in age
and wealth, he knows that only ritual can grant
his wish, and enlists to enact the elaborate service
a priest with a skilled and liquid tongue. A stallion
as clean as an infant's conscience is paraded like a monstrance
through the kingdom of Ayodhya. It's led to the templed ring
of his courtyard and tied to a central golden stake
where the wood of sacrifice is piled in preparation.
The blaze is lit while each word is recited in accurate
cadence. The horse writhes in the rampant red frenzy
of flame, suffers the savage inhuman pain, and falls,
the victim of a fatherly wish. The prayer
plucks the strings of the universe's nerves;
Dasaratha awaits the small gift of himself.

Ravana, the ten-headed demon of Lanka, is poised
to topple the temples of heaven,
rip all the rich fabric from the backs of the gods,
and reduce them to his abject band of servants.
Ravana, as a boon from the sleep-infested Brahma,
had asked immunity from the hands of the gods,
and now only a human can arrest his pillage.
In the cerulean of the gods' near-eternal assembly,
Vishnu, the source and preserver of the Earth,
is eager for adventures in the world he dreams,
that curls like smoke from his smooth blue nostrils.

Curious to be stripped of his godly knowledge
and find relief from the tedious pleasures of heaven,
he hankers for plain human learning and oblivion.
Invited to step into the story he's made,
he's as eager as a child to make himself small
and submit to a scale his large self can't see.
To preserve the world in all its bright branches
he descends like a tumbling chunk of the sky.

There's a hush and a reek of burning hair that can never
be expunged from the nostrils' memory. The priest
and his thousand meticulous attendants have deftly
picked the lock of heaven's treasury. A giant as blinding red
as sunset, his body a rippling column of fire, stands in flames
that stink of screaming horse. He holds
the god-seed in a bowl in his hands, a gold
bowl crowned with a lid of silver. He holds it
as angels hold gifts of white lilies, offers the smooth
blue pudding to the king, who feeds it to the mouths
    and wombs
of his wives. Half goes to the faithful Mary-mother Kausalya,
the rest to two others, to Kaikeyi and Sumitra,
who will bear him three sons, Sumitra's portion
dividing inside her. The fractional god
is mathed out through the family, and the king
becomes cuckold to Vishnu's virility.

His wives take the cool blue pudding on their tongues:
it tastes like the honey of sky-blue bees,
like the feasts of love that had bubbled in their brains.
Swelling each with the fetus of heaven's blue food,
they grow in secret like the smile of stars.

Kausalya bears the bright and wise-eyed Rama,
a boy who alights in the blue of his skin.
His three brothers are born in rapid succession
and the breasts of their mothers feed the small mouths
as god divided arrives in the world.

II

Rama Wins Sita

For years I've practised the keen arts of war – can launch
an arrow further than any of my brothers, or any
of the warriors who taught me their skill And still
my shafts pierce precisely their mark. But in these ten days
of illusion and conquest I've grown more to manhood
than in sixteen years. A rustic monk entered
the splendour of the palace, and his face held a power
older than my father's. He asked the king for my help
to rid his shrine of the demon that befouls his sacrifices
with breath-halting gusts of shrieking and stench.
Of demons I knew only what I'd heard in stories:
their merciless butchery and their biting out the beating
of a good man's heart. Now, with the reluctant
blessing of my father, I was the prince who sets out
to destroy one. My brother Lakshmana went with me,
as always, walking beside me as my second self, the mirror
and ferry of all of my thoughts. Vishvamitra taught us mantras,
weapons of prayer, the acrobatic leapings between heaven
and war. We bound our minds to him as our teacher.

In our days of preparation we lived with the monks. We slept
on the uncushioned bed of the earth, wore clothes of bark, ate
unseasoned grains, and were admitted to their spinning
    rhythms
of prayer. Here I entered a life
as pure as a story and tasted, like the hidden
flavour of water, the one source my life cannot be without.
I sampled with their tea the wild honey of my dreams
and was stung by the hunger for a holy man's days. My mind
released its own subtle scent of devotion,

and here in the cool holy shade of the forest
my flesh was infused with the petals of prayer.

The demon that needed to be killed was female,
and the swords of our mantras were drawn in our minds.
When our offering to the gods was precisely prepared, she like a
    raptor
bore down upon us. Neither of us had ever set eyes on such
wild and unscrupulous feminine beauty, on breasts and hips
    that itched
our eyes and swayed like a mesmerist over our wills.
She set a screen like magic before her, wrapped in mist
as decoying fabric, and from within it she aimed her arrows
to kill us. Vishvamitra tugged us from reverie, ordered us not
to regard her as a woman; and our aim
was set. The arrow that ended her
was shot from my bow, released in fine anger
with consummate strength. And before us
was a woman's corrupted carcass, her breasts collapsed
like oozing melons, and each of her features
putrid on her face, her flesh
seething and bruised as worm-eaten fruit.

And I was Vishvamitra's well-prized champion.
After the ritual had at last been performed,
each phrase and vessel ringing clearly in its place,
he told us as a blessing we'd travel to Mithila,
where the king keeps the world's most enormous bow
that once belonged to the potent Lord Shiva.
The holy man told me, like a medal for my skill,
of the king of Mithila's marvellous daughter,
so lovely that princes had besieged the city,
each requesting the favour of her hand.
But the king had proclaimed that his daughter would marry

only the man who could master Shiva's bow.
I had set out on this story and could taste my part.

The bow was more massive than I had imagined,
wheeled out to the courtyard by dozens of men.
No human in history had been able to lift it,
far less make it bend to the shape of his will.
There in the centre of the eight-sided square
I lifted it easily as a needed sword;
Lakshmana and all the crowd were hushed.
I bent it till it took the shape of the moon,
till my muscles had nearly met their match,
and the string all but met the tip of the bow.
Then with a thunderous report it broke;
the weapon of Shiva was fractured in my hands
and I stood like a god before that assembly.

Now, as reward, I'll be given Sita.
I try to picture her invisible beauty,
misted by the words of all who extol her.
I know nothing of the workings in the egg of marriage,
but as a sadhu learns to lay his sacrifice
and recite the intricate evocations of the gods,
I will learn the order of my life with Sita.

III

Sita Weds Rama

I step round the fire beside you, my lord,
and again round the fire to wed you, my lord.

You, the blue tiger prowling my dreams,
have returned to pluck me from my father's side,

dispersing the suitors who vied for my hand,
who watched and were dashed as you snapped Shiva's bow.

You are the peacock who startled from slumber
all of my mild-faced bevy of women;

you drew me from chambers where I lounged with my sisters,
and called me with all your broad-shouldered beauty.

You've stepped to the palace as a god steps to the ground,
and your skin is blue with the scent of the sky.

I am the fatherless daughter of Earth,
sprung from fresh-furrowed moist dark soil

when my father, his mind a ploughshare of prayer,
opened for sacrifice a fallow field.

We are the story of marrying worlds:
blue drops of heaven on the thirsting Earth.

This glistening sari is the life-work of women
whose fingers for years have advanced to this day;

decked in gems that would shame the stars,
I am melted to you, a jewel of blue.

You are the smooth-skinned phrase of consummation
that waits like a sweet at the close of my story.

I step round the fire to wed you, my lord,
and again round the fire beside you, my lord.

IV

Rama is Banished

Newly wed, they return to the city of Ayodhya,
and enjoy honeymoon months in the capital's devotion. Soon
it's announced that Rama will be crowned. On the day
    Dasaratha
will abdicate his title and invest his son with his glittering
    future,
Kaikeyi – mother of Rama's brother Bharata
and Dasaratha's one sexually indispensable wife –
lies writhing in her dark red room of anger. As sly
and treacherous as Rebecca, she's determined to steal
a blessing for her son and trick
her husband into unretractable words. She'll collect
on the boons Dasaratha promised when she –
on the battlefield years before – snatched back his life,
and carried her husband's torn body from war, saving him from
    the crush
of elephants' feet. In the following gust of gratitude, he had
    promised
whatever she might ask. The fairy clock had begun to tick.

He's informed that his wife lies twisting in fury in the room
with walls as scarlet as her heart's. Distraught by upheaval
on the day of coronation and eager to assuage his sweetheart's
    rage,
he enters and entreats her to reveal the source of her injury. He
    agrees
to perform whatever she asks, and swears this by Rama, the
    treasure
of his age, without whom he could not live a day.
Her own son, Bharata, to take the throne
and Rama banished to the forest for fourteen years.

A white horse has planted its hooves
on his lungs. He bows
as a king must to the rigours of his word. In the noose
of his promise, Dasaratha accepts.

Seeking blessing on the day of his ascension, Rama enters
the grandeur of his father's broad chamber. He scans the wealth
and the servants that will soon be his burden. Dasaratha, face
    broken
like a fine painted plate, tells his son how his softness to his
    wife
has destroyed him. He condemns his blue hope to the long
    years of exile
while tears stream down the fissures of his face. A dutiful son,
Rama calmly assents, reassuring his father his promise must be
    kept,
the one glass bowl of his word preserved. Lakshmana
    reasonably
seeks to argue a reprieve, is silenced
by the resolve in Rama's eyes. They leave their father
alone with his throne in a bath of grief that cannot
but destroy him. Rama orders his weapons stored
for his return, his princely robes folded in deep
scented chests, and arranges Sita's placement in Bharata's care.

He returns to their home and addresses his wife
on the day that she was to be installed as queen:
"There's no need to prepare for today's coronation.
My father, keeping his solemn word to Kaikeyi,
will place my beloved Bharata on the throne
and consign me to the forest for fourteen years.
I will go, as each aspirant goes, alone,
and live like the ascetics whose rites I defended,
the monks who hold treasures of inestimable worth.

You will be safe, well-protected in the city.
I've obtained Bharata's promise to provide you
with the women and allowance and indulgence you require
so your life will not lack any luxury or wish.
I ask you to bear this as a quiet sacrifice
and watch patiently as I will for the day of my return."

He is pleased with his speech but perceives her sorrow;
his heart is swelling with separation; he adds:
"I will still adore you each day of my exile,
and strew the petals of my words at your distant feet."

Sita feels the cool trickle of sweat between her breasts.
Her mind is a lime cut cleanly in two:
here, the comforts and fabrics that have made her herself,
the jewels, the delicacies, the innumerable servants,
the women she's lived with for all of her days;
there, the prince whose promise makes her whole.
She sees she is no one if not his wife.
She declares that she will go anywhere with him,
but cannot face a life that is not by his side.
The forest, he warns, is no place for a princess:
there scraping thorns and sharp-toothed beasts
take the place of silk cushions and peacocks in gardens;
wild and simple unflavoured roots
supplant the spiced dishes served at the palace.
She will not be coddled at the cost of his presence.
"Kill me," she says, "if you would sever me from you."
He is wounded, bewildered, his solicitude not recognized.
He accepts her accompaniment on the path of his exile
with a shadow of the alacrity with which he accepted
the following of his faithful servant-brother Lakshamana,
the one he'd take even when departing alone.

Rama's quickly ready to dress his new part, strips
and dons an ascetic's coarse costume, a simple garment
that still highlights his beauty. Sita is simply unable
to undress, would not know herself without her fine clothing,
drapes a robe like a sack over princess's fashions, steps
toward the forest like tearing fabric; Rama leads her
as Hansel leads Gretel to the woods. He demonstrates the
    patience
of the ascetics who taught him, who watch slow saplings shade
into trees. He has seen in the tragedy of the day's unravelling
a man of his father's nobility and wisdom
enslaved to his desires for an earthly woman.
Taking his leave from his father and city,
he's ready for the romance of separation from Sita.

V

The Abduction of Sita

They set up house in the heart of the forest,
Lakshmana assembling a near-comfortable cottage
from the forest's abundance of creeper and tree.
He clears a path to the stream, paves it with stones,
transplants the bright flowers that delight Sita's eyes.

Meanwhile lust stirs on a far southern island.
Fed by his familial network of informants,
Ravana, the ten-headed demon of Lanka,
has heard word of Sita's unparalleled beauty
and set his sights on the exquisite princess.
He will win her with illusion and removal of men.
His magician like Vishnu takes on a new shape,
claims power by stepping down creation's ladder
and entering the sleek silver hide of a deer.
It flashes its emerald horns by the stream
where Sita like Persephone has strayed for flowers.
She's enamoured of the deer's swift leaping thigh,
the glint of its quick and sapphire hooves.
She craves it like silk and the adulation of suitors
in this wilderness that yields neither finery nor jewels.
Deep already in infatuation's forest,
she will hear no talk of any illusion,
of a demon's magician in a hart's fine hide,
dismisses all Lakshmana's attempts to dissuade her –
the words of this man who knows nothing of women.
Sita can sulk as beautifully as the moon,
a princess pampered with the thick jam of praise.
She encircles herself in the curtains of her whim,
enlists her blue husband to indulge her desire,

sends her archer to fetch her a pet or a rug;
Lakshmana, silenced, is ordered to protect her.

Rama enters the woods, blind dupe of the demon
who leads his feet through a labyrinth of wildness,
and knots the elaborate fine lines of this noose.
When finally Rama sights the glinting beast,
he lays arrow to string, lets in plunge to the deer
and drive deep into flesh with the sound he adores.
His arrow pierces deception's heart,
tricking the lock that turned demon to beauty
and releasing the graceless stench of bad death.
There's no hide but only a demon's rank skin.
The last words that wind from the magician's mouth
are a carefully volleyed lasso of deceit,
a ventriloquist's plea in dumb Rama's own voice.
"Lakshmana," it pleads, "help me – I've fallen."
Lakshmana, unmarried and wise in the ways of demons,
suspects the ploy to leave Sita unmanned,
informs her that this is a stratagem of demons,
that Rama's in no danger; he'll remain by her side.
Sita is frantic that Rama may be lost,
and Lakshmana the faithful is slapped on both cheeks.
She pummels on his head every curse she has heard,
calls him hater of his brother, luster for his wife,
a lecher who would nibble unhindered on her beauty
and see his own brother devoured by beasts.
She shames him into seeking Rama in the forest.

She waits like Snow White alone in the cottage,
a ripe berry of innocence, beauty, and greed.
Disguised in a sumptuous young man's body
beneath the saffron of a holy man's robes,
Ravana advances in a silence of birdsong.

He invites Sita from her cottage to consider his words,
praises her shapeliness, her slender waist,
the royal and generous curve of her lips,
her eyes that lure him to drown in devotion.
He invites her to be his amorous consort.
Not entirely unwelcome are such words
here where only Rama gives voice to her beauty.
But she is the wife of a prince, she tells him,
not a whore to be plucked with a few choice words
or the coarse hands of a man who forages in the woods.
Ravana grows impatient with this courtly game,
won't continue to stroke her with flattering phrases.
He explodes at once to his full demon height,
swells like a witch from out of his disguise,
sprouting ten heads and twenty muscled arms,
each as thick as the strongest of snakes.
He rapes her hair, curls it like rings around his fingers,
the hundred he'd spider over her skin
as he'd feast his full ten mouths on her flesh,
probing with his tongues the taste of her pores.
Hurled like a sack of produce or game,
she's dumped in his chariot, pulled to the sky,
feels her insides left somewhere beneath her.
Unsupported, without husband or ground to stand on,
she dispenses the treasure she's carried like a second skin.
Spying five solemn monkeys on the peak of a mountain,
she bundles in silk her own finest jewels,
the closest she has to a signet or seal,
and, unseen by Ravana, drops this parcel toward them.

VI

Rama and Sita, Separated

My Sita is lost in Ravana's fortress;
my love is lost beyond the kingdom of the monkeys.

> Before me a thousand demons and servants;
> before me, my Rama, I see only you.

The lotus and waterfalls speak only of Sita;
the eyes of the deer point only to her.

> You are the cloak and guardian of my hours,
> the one memory that shields my skin from shame.

Without Sita the sun is torn from my eyes,
and I'm warmed by a light I can only imagine.

> You are the tiger who blazes and scatters his enemies;
> like my father you'll save me from the tumult of dreams.

At the sight of Sita my skin burned with blue flame,
and my body betrayed me like the glistening of honey.

> You brought me the deep sweet taste of darkness,
> wild water running with scents of night.

She has risen like swans as they stroke through the air.
She has startled my feet and lips into reverence.

> You are the lord who'll fight oceans to find me,
> scorn sleep till you take me again in your arms.

Like an eagle she has spread her wings and ascended
to the great and sky-blue summit of my thought.

 I wait for your skin as the cover of evening,
  the blue black young night and the light of stars.

To her I would light a thousand bright lamps.
For her I would cross the dark channel of dreams.

VII

Rama in the Monsoon Season

Again I've displayed my prowess as a warrior and secured
the alliance of the monkey king. Now, as he lounges
entwined with his wives, I share the hard floor of this cave
with my brother, eating nothing more delicate than what food
he can forage, and sitting the long and patient vigil
for Sita, the one woman surpassing any born on Earth.

Sita has become as lovely as a lotus, and I
could feed on her petals forever. I must wait
for fair weather until I retrieve her, until we can assemble
an army and advance, win my shrine that has fallen
into infidel hands. The earth is furrowed and softened with
    showers,
rain slides like mantras over my days, and in pauses

of rain there's the sluice of the waterfall, there
in the morning and at night when I wake: she calls to my heart
in the cool rush of water, in the patter and hiss
and soft dripping of rain. In my prayers she is peaceful,
and so she must be: smiling, beatific, through curtains
of rain, showering my eyes with the mist of her vision.

Some mornings this rescue feels as foolish as gold: battling
    demons
for what I already possess. Had I ever before
heard rain water trickling and known it was cleaning the roots
of my brain? Her departure has fed this liquid conversion;
my earlier tastes were blunt, as a monkey's, as easily fed
by mere parcels of flesh. Now I cherish the woman who distils

all women, who has shed like a snake her woman's skin.
I will wake in a season to my princely life. It's my duty
to reclaim every hair that's been stolen, to trounce
the demon who's snatched her from me, to return to my side
her plundered body. Brothered with Lakshmana I will conquer
Ravana and establish my name as the greatest of warriors.

Here are the jewels which were dropped from heaven,
which the monkey king, Sugriva, placed in my hand.
They are as pellucid as the memory of her eyes, like crystal
fitted to the form of her skin, the icons that stand
at the centre of this shrine. They are the relics that dwelt
on her flesh when she lived in this world as my earthly wife.

In place of her flesh she has sent her cool spirit that arcs
like the swans that glide after rain. I pray to her beauty
as I'd pray to the rich unseen light of the moon,
more lovely occluded by the clouds of monsoon.
I've learned why ascetics are devoted to blindness,
to caves where the memory of sight is made clean.

The Earth with all her tresses is drenched, streams
running fresh down the shoulders of mountains. Sita –
like the queen of heaven in the finest of saris –
steps down with washed feet to sprinkle her blessings
and bathe me in the radiance of all her great calm.
It rains and for months will continue to rain.

VIII

Sita in the Garden

There remain two months before Ravana will dismember me,
have me spiced and stewed by his excellent chefs,
savoured by each of his ten eager mouths.
Ten months ago now, I was dragged like a whore
to his chariot and taken, an exile from exile,
to this garden walled within this walled city,
on this island of Lanka, half the earth from my home.
Has Rama forgotten me? Why does he not come?
Where now is the lord who swore to defend me?
Do his delicate eyes so loathe my visage
that he would prefer empty air to my face?
Cannot the strongest and wisest of men
find me and snatch me from Ravana's jaws?
My sari that I've worn for three hundred days
is as soiled and torn as that of a slattern.
My face that he praised as the luminous moon
is unwashed, unpainted, thick with grease,
smeared with the crusting rivers of tears.
My hair, once smooth and oiled as the curtains of night,
is all uncombed, forms mats and knots,
carries clumps like the hives of prickling insects.

A monster has taken me deep to the south,
to a world beneath the world I knew.
A serpent stronger than the gods themselves,
Ravana comes as a courter, a wooer, a prince,
praises my figure and the light of my eyes.
He forgets I'm an animal he's placed in a cage.
He assaults me again with his talk of marriage,
and I scent like a knife my wedding to Rama:

being held like a splendid cup in hands
I thought would treasure and revere me forever.

When Ravana leaves me, two months to my stewing,
in the garden of demon guards and flowers,
among the still delicious scent of mangoes,
I take refuge beneath a tree of gold.
And now the tree speaks like the tree of a dream.
It tells me the story I most love to hear as my mind
is unfolding and tumbling toward sleep: How once
in the magnificent city of Ayodhya there was born a blue-
    skinned
prince named Rama, who grew in strength, a tiger
among men, who shattered Shiva's bow like kindling
to win the jewelled prize of Mithila's daughter, who
chased the sapphire-hoofed deer for his wife, lamented her loss
as the loss of the moon, begged trees to tell him
where he might find her, won from armies of monkeys,
baboons, and bears their oaths of allegiance in rescuing
Sita, who sent me, his devoted,
faithful servant, here to the island of Lanka
to find you. Snatches, discontinuous, scenes
of a dream. And which voice among me is this one who speaks?

The dream voice is a monkey the size of a cat,
a monkey perched still in the branches above me.
I have fallen to a world where monkeys recite and smiling
cat-creatures speak from gold trees. But is he not
another of Ravana's sly demons who's assumed a shape
and a story to seduce me? "I am Hanuman,"
he tells me, "son of the wind god; doubt me no more:
I am Hanuman." It's as if my body were yielding
to a breeze. He holds in his deft almost human paw
a gift I can't bear to lose on waking: the smooth gold,

the eye-flash of Rama's own hand, the ring that adorned
and circled his finger as he once encircled and enclosed my days.

The cat-monkey offers to carry me home,
to deliver me to Rama if I'll climb on his back.
For the first time in months my body can laugh.
"Look at your tininess, you could not carry me
any more than a mouse could carry a tigress."
He swells to a monkey of enormous size,
nearly stooping beneath the blue ceiling of the sky.
"Oh no, but still I could not," I add,
half-turning to avert my face from him
(I am, I remind us both, a princess).
"It would be improper for me – would it not?—
to touch any male who is not my husband."
And I am back in my place in the story,
a princess who waits for her prince to come.
I hold his ring, and this kind-hearted Hanuman,
the nearest to my beloved I've seen for months,
leaves to summon him, my invincible lord,
and restore me to all the honour of his wife.

IX

The Rain of Snakes

Rama's forces are pitched beyond the walls of Lanka:
serried ranks of monkeys, gold, russet, and white; bears
from far kingdoms and soldiering baboons. Combatants on
    both sides
have been pierced to their deaths. Today,
the rain on Rama's army is snakes:
arrows unleashed from all points in the sky, missiles whose
    source
cannot be aimed at, prayed against,
stopped. They pour like undulating ribbons of night,
    blackening
the heavens with pharaonic plague. They deliver
a death of burning coolness, slick
strands sliding reptilian on the skin, roasting
in fever the bodies where they breed. Warriors are felled,
their skin half-eclipsed beneath magnified
maggots that feed on their flesh. Beside
the dim cadaver that must be Lakshmana, with sliding
jewelled bands about his blue arms, and a face
like a weakening mirror
of sky, is Rama, the conqueror,
snake-shamed and still.

Indrajit, Ravana's son and right-hands man, has drawn
on his infinite quiver of snakes. He wears invisibility
like borrowed breath and moves, imperceptible death,
through the air. Flying swift as demon thought to the palace,
he approaches his father's stolen trophy, picks her up
for this one illicit date. He thinks her beauty almost evil,
and wants it. He escorts her aboard the family aircraft,
the Puspaka chariot stolen from the treasury of the gods,

its magical gadgetry sure to impress her
and add to her sense of his dazzling worth. He leads her up
staircases crusted with emeralds
to a viewing deck bordered with diamonds and gold,
where thrones give a god's-eye view of the world. Directing
the machinery with the levers of his mind, banking
and looping to impress the girl, Indrajit
guides the Puspaka's course. Proudly he displays
the field of his carnage, the teeming
corruption of the numbers he's murdered, the extent
by which he's exceeded this beauty's dead husband.
Sita watches, like Helen from the ramparts of Troy,
the gore that is born from one beautiful face.
And there, like shards of lapis lazuli,
lies the shattered body of her world, her Rama.
The hands of her face are frozen
in this moment. She feels the breath
of her lungs escape her,
her story burned back
to the roots of its start. That she
had been minced to a demon's meal
before being consumed by such a sight.
The ring she'd hung round her neck
with rough twine now melts
from hope into slow-burning memory.
She is not Rama's wife. She is not.
The Puspaka chariot returns
to Lanka, weighted almost
beyond its magic by the imploded
star of Sita's heart.

There can be no hope but an animal rescue.
The eagle Garuda, the vehicle of Vishnu
and the swirling St. Patrick of the avian world,

swoops as a hero to the reddened field.
Garuda – the insuperable antidote to serpents,
before whom they flee like quick braided dreams –
paints his wide shadow over the battlefield.
Before he lands it is vacant of snakes,
holds only the audible memory of their sliding.
Garuda strokes his pinions on Ayodhya's prince,
restoring Rama's bleak organs to wholeness,
his skin to the smoothness and scent of blue milk.
He dusts and soothes and heals the innards,
the limbs of fallen men, bears, and monkeys.
He barely hears their grateful, worshipful words
before again ascending to his watch in the sky.

Sita, collapsed beneath the tree that's her home,
has seen the death of her husband and lived.

X

Rama Looks on Sita's Death

Lying in the cool twisting sleep of snakes,
I woke to find my brother beside me dead,
his body all lepered by Indrajit's shafts.
With my heart's-blood stolen by the snakes of war,
I would have bid Sugriva send home his troops,
for victory unbrothered could hold no sweetness.

Even if Sita were lost to me then I'd live
in her radiance daily in prayer and know her
more purely than ever I had. But without Lakshmana,
the one whose tongue treads as light as my thought
and whose words are the counsel of my truest mind,
I would be no more than the fraction of a man.

When Garuda returned the life of my brother,
stroking his broken corpse with soft feathers,
caressing his body and leaving me whole,
I was given my one inoculation against death.
When Hanuman explodes upon us with the news
I perceive the scene clear and religious as a painting.

He has seen Sita captive in Indrajit's chariot,
watched the sword raised to her swan-like throat.
How ravishing, appalling is the picture detailed
by the words of Hanuman's tear-licked mouth:
her bright severed skin leaving Indrajit's blade,
her scarlet life draped and gorgeous on her sari.

She glistens with the quick surging colours of her heart,
garlanded with each of her braids of blood.
How exquisitely her beauty is transfixed on his sword,
the moon of her sublimity flooded with blood.
I fall like a tree in an ecstasy of grief,
my brain's thousand branches thundering with light.

Lakshmana, the voice of all love and reserve,
tells me it's a trick of Indrajit's magic,
assures me that again it's the deceit of demons,
an illusion to slaughter our last resolve:
that Indrajit's too smitten with Sita's fine figure
to carve up the body of his love like a pig.

Whatever is illusion, I know my own vision:
Hanuman's picture muralled on my mind,
my soul washed in the falling of Sita's blood
as her spirit is lifted to the refuge of heaven.
She's enclosed now in all the cold blue of the sky,
and her image in my heart is impregnably safe.

XI

The Sacrifice of Sita

A jubilant Hanuman meets Sita in the grove.
He announces that she is now free
of Ravana. Her champion of a husband
has reduced him to legend: dispatching his life
with an arrow from Brahma. "Rama wishes," delivers
    Hanuman,
"to see you as his bride." She submits to be bathed
by her demon attendants. They slowly, painfully
comb out her hair till it's as smooth as a river
on a moonlit night. They scent her skin to prepare her
for Rama, clothe her in a sari as lovely as a wedding,
and accompany her in the palanquin that takes her to him.
When she is laden again as a princess,
strung as a bride with the weight of jewels,
she knows he will never hear her history,
regard her in grief, her face smeared with grease,
her sari the taunt of the rakshasa women.
She's primped for her role in his costume drama.
She must hide him like a child from her vileness and grime.
She would rather have walked to him barefoot and filthy
than ride like a new, second wife in a cavalcade,
her face clean and smooth as the silent moon.
She no longer wishes to be displayed as a treasure,
or parade as his beauty queen prize through the streets.

Sita's told that Rama will receive her in public,
disregarding her wishes. She walks toward him
down an aisle of stone. She steps, nearly breathless,
beneath the eyes of thousands, their gauntlet of looks.
More than one is murmuring, "Whore."
She hears someone spit. She is the woman

caught in an adultery she didn't commit.
She keeps her eyes fixed on the pavement before her.
When she sees the dear blue feet of Rama
her eyes rise slowly till she takes in his face. She's tossed
from blank anger to the memory of marriage, her
indignation subverted by the old tug of love.

But the blue face of Rama is poised and unmoved.
He has hurried her into the Antinous of his heart,
needs her absence so he might worship her image.
He begins a prepared and public speech.
Sita feels blisters rising on the surface of her heart.
"I have won you from Ravana and restored my honour,
shown that acts against me will be fiercely avenged,
that I am no soldier or prince to be slighted.
I wish that I could also redeem your honour,
but that, regrettably, lies beyond my power.
For nearly ten years you have kept yourself
as a guest in the palace of a shameless demon
who could not have left your beauty untouched,
the channels of your body clean and unentered.
Your flesh has been tainted beyond any cleansing,
and I cannot uphold virtue with you by my side.
The gross desecration of your body offends me.
You are no longer mine. You may go where you please."

Sita shakes with waves of injustice,
the dark red paint of public shame. She is not
a wife to be dispensed with. Her words
strike Rama with a smart on his cheek:
"There is no other man
to whom I could go. As you will not receive me –
I will enter the fire. Please, my lord, a pyre."

Lakshmana, Rama's conscience bent to his will,
collects the wood and sets the fire.
Sita, with an athlete's intense
concentration, prepares herself to enter
the flames. Strengthened by the years with no man
to uphold her, she prays to Agni,
god of sacrifice and fire, that he
will show Rama where faithfulness lies. She steps
to the crackling torch of her trial, like the three
young men thrown into Nebuchadnezzar's
furnace, all cool and uncombusted by leaping heat. She walks
upon embers as over silk cushions, dancing it seems
in the elegance of flames. The crowd
is silent. Rama pales to a watery
blue. Sita steps from her victory lap in the furnace, each thread
of her sari, each ornament unsinged.

Rama feels his army's eyes upon him.
This is a scene he did not prepare lines for. He descends
from his throne, approaches Sita, needing to embrace her
but fearing himself scorched. Her arms encircle
Rama's body, and they are uneasily coupled in public.
They'll return to Rama's native Ayodhya and receive
the throne from his regent brother Bharata. Rama
the warrior has been subject to his consort,
and Sita is more fully than ever alive.

XII

Rama Banishes Sita

When she'd stepped from the flames he was vastly betrayed,
unable to think what her skin might be made of.
Now he will always detest and adore her,
his finest thoughts chafed by the silk of her skin.

He's Pygmalion wishing his woman back to stone,
desiring her return to cool marble and silence:
the figure his prayers had carved for years
shattered by the movement of her limbs and tongue.

For one as lofty in his thoughts as Rama
the absence of a woman can make her divine.
For years he had lived without his Sita,
and she was already Lakshmi in his mind.

Rama has been tortured by the touch of prayer,
and his counsellors cannily read his desires.
When, some months later in the chambers of Ayodhya,
they mutter complaints of their faithless wives

who see his Sita as their leader in crime,
he employs his position to cleanse the nation.
"For the good of a well-ordered state," he says,
as he forfeits the plate of his conjugal pleasure

and consigns his wife to the dark of the forest.
His goddess's body has hampered his vision,
and he retreats from heaven's invasion of his senses
to the paintings still radiant at the back of his eyes.

He speaks to his faithful servant Lakshmana,
who's learned resolute and unflinching obedience
and adopted the saintly silence of a wife.
He tells him Sita's example must be erased.

Lakshmana bears it like the weight of firewood.
Like the huntsman leading Snow White to the woods,
he accompanies Sita to the forest's ashrams,
leaving her there in a pool of his tears.

XIII

Sita in the Forest

The twins set out for their lessons with Valmiki. They sit
attentive at the temple of his knees, hearing the history
of the world and themselves, learning to recite in well-metred
    words
the violence and the suffering by which they were born.
Their voices stir the very stones into listening.
I too pass some of my evenings with the sage, and he hears
me tell the worn story of Rama. The history
shines clear in the waters of his mind as he tailors
our story to the truth of verse.
Kusa and Lava grow proudly into boys, dressing up
in the heroic clothing of their father, playing Rama
and the demons as they hide among trees.

For the hours they're away I spin time with the women.
We don't pray as the men do, intent on sacrifice, but
more the way mothers pray to their children, addressing
    ourselves
to the hope of the gods, and invoking the goddess
who boldly, unswervingly stares men in the face.
We pray to the half-trampled flowers of ourselves.
My story here is one among many
of men who jealously spat fire on our skin; of women
scorned when their bodies betrayed them, or accused
of adultery of idea or belief, of dishonouring
their fathers with their masculine words.

What we do is not lofty or worthy of envy.
The circle of our days is that of all women
who know nothing but the ritual of feeding the world.
We keep it clean and clothed and breathing,

and embroider it quietly with beauty's small flowers.
We feed the ashram's physical hungers,
miming great pandits and girls playing house.
I've recalled the fine dishes served in the palace
when the kingdom was arrayed like baubles at my feet,
wondered at the craft that led to such flavours.
Now I wish for no more than this day's simple food,
and my mind is nearly swept clean of temptations.
I have circled the fire in fine clothes with my groom,
and sat on the throne of his kingdom beside him.
Now I'm a woman who lays her own fires,
who darkens her hands with cinder and ash,
labouring with half-sisters to cook and sew.

We listen to the Vedas and feel them runnelling our skin,
forming lines of smiles that gather round our eyes.
I know myself weighted to the land who bore me,
am learning gravity's great seduction and embrace.
As a mother I'm sinking back to love with my mother, melting
to the ease of Earth's body at night, yielding to the strength
of women's arms, and cooled by the low soft lapping of their
    tongues.
I would soak to the filtering ground of my mother to grow
like a vegetal dream of the world and stretch to each pore
of the Earth's dark skin. I want to be no one
but Earth's gift of richness, carrying baskets
and provisions from my mother's great store.

My sons advance in age and knowledge, never quite bury
the story I've told them in the elegant lines Valmiki recites.
I'm there in their language like a woman in the soil.

XIV

The Descent of Sita

Two boys are sent to the king with their story. They call it
Ramayana, Rama's Journey, and tell it like a river
snaking in their veins. Rama sits paired with his brother
    Lakshmana
in the public assembly where the twins recite. He hears them
    telling
a tale half his, but belonging also
to Sita and the gods, and the eye of the poet
who imagined its scenes: all the fractions
form inaccurate sums. He sees his own face
doubled before him, himself in miniature
with eloquent tongues, the duplicate children who fragment his
    mind.
He meets his sons, who tell him like spies
the plot of his life. He, the clear hero of this epic tale,
is a stain that spreads beneath their words, and ignominy
burrows beneath his robes. There's no fault to be found
in the adulation of their speech, but their words
keep slipping from the plates they're told on. He perceives
cool Sita like a lizard on his skin.
Valmiki attests that these are his children and proclaims as a
    prophet
that Sita is chaste. The murmuring
crowd determines his action. Cold justice demands
he recall her from exile. And he's stirred
by some musty vague remnant
of lust. Offering Valmiki his generous reward,
Rama commands him to summon Sita. But she will not
    succumb
to the air of the palace, or endure the grandeur

of Rama's roof. She requests a meeting
in the open-air fields outside of Ayodhya.

Before him she stands as the inscrutable moon.
She is plain in her beauty and no longer his.
She is naked of all her jewels:
they lie forgotten in a basket in her hut
or where they were tossed among the playthings of her sons.
Having borne her twins like Rapunzel in exile
she submits them now to their father's care:
to Rama who will with assurance claim them,
and Lakshmana who'll stand as their second parent.
Taught by the forest and the stories of their mother,
by the measured, complaisant lines of Valmiki,
they'll hear the official tongue of their father
and be trained as princes in governance and war.
They hardly look back. Her work is complete.

When she speaks it's not to the man who was her husband
but her mother, the sturdy, unimpeachable Earth:
"I turn to you as leaves turn softly to soil,
salute you as the one steady source of my breath.
For years I've longed for you to invite my return,
longed to melt in the sureness of your easeful embrace.
I have played out my parts as woman and mother
with all the care and devotion I've known,
and extended the blessing of your life to my sons.
If I've kept the promise of my fatherless birth,
and been tuned to the rhythms and codes of your motion,
may you now draw me again to your breast
to join you in dispensing prosperity's flowers."

Rama watches her, frightened, bewildered.

"If I have been faithful to you," she says,
"may your strong arms again enfold me."
Rama hears her words addressed to him,
and thinks that she is still talking about sex.

Sita hums the soft tune of her mother's embrace, roots and
    vines
lace themselves round her feet, and she sinks
to the simmering stew of the Earth. He watches her swallowed
by slow hungry soil. He watches the solid world flooding
her feet, foaming as the rising
speckled tide at her knees, wrapping her to the waist
in its rich dark skirt. She tumbles like Persephone in her own
chosen chariot, driving herself to the bosom of the Earth. She's
    received
by the loamy arms of her mother, feels her skin breathing
a rare dark air, and hears fading behind her
the sharp cries of Rama.

He pours out his heart in rehearsed lamentation,
rends the fabric of his former life.
He exults in the blessings attendant on her death,
and embraces his work of praise and proclamation.
Calmly as a prayerbook in the hands of a priest,
his mind is turning to the page of this grief.

XV

Rama Redacting

As a sadhu I rise to my morning of prayer. I touch my
forehead with dirt her feet have made holy, and press her bright
    image
on the screen of my eyes. She has opened in my chest a clear
column of air, shaped it by the touch of her gentlest fingers,
and filled it with the flourish of unearthly song.

Daily I labour to edit her sayings, her aphorisms,
teachings, and snatches of verse. I seek her immaculate
voice beneath accretions, transforming the memories of others,
and my own, to syllables rounded as pebbles in a river,
truths that brush vivid religion on the mind.

Here in this court in the guise of a king, I live
as no more than Sita's apostle, smoothing the half-
polished jewels of her deeds. As naked of thought
as a poet or prophet, I listen for the whispering
of her words on the air, and pen them unerringly

on the pages of my brain. I, the one whom Sita loved,
perceive her more clearly than any who heard her: than women
who blankly recited her verses or children without
articulate memory. I cast into apocrypha all her false
gospels as a gardener tugs out each of heresy's weeds.

Her spirit guides the pen through my unworthy hand and
    gathers
the words that were tossed on old paper, recasts them
as water shines stones into light. The speech of Sita
must be diamonds at night, must be scent of lotus
on river breezes, sentences feathered as songbird and fern.

Her breath swells my heart with abundance of phrases,
leads my hand to delight in rare species of beauty. Like
a pitcher of dreams and the rich rain of heaven, Sita bestows
the cool blessing of her lines, and I know in the snailing curve
of my ear the words she releases like chimes of blue air.

XVI

Rama and Sita as Vishnu and Lakshmi

After centuries composing herself in the Earth,
immersed in the spinning chrysalis of prayer
and practising the seasons' repeated revolutions;
stained by the complex pigments of the planet
and hearing in her skin her mother's old stories,
her dreams of coupling, divergence, profusion;
from the darkness of soil Sita's birthed into heaven,
and steps as Lakshmi to the cushions of clouds.

Rama, after shaping the stories of Sita,
leaves the clear text of her life as his opus.
Immersed in the current of his final cold river,
he submits to the death of a priestly old king.
He rides the swift elevator up into heaven,
and slips back to the shape of Vishnu's absence.
He's received as a hero by his cohort of gods,
and his mind is wiped clear as cool blue glass.

They face each other through pale bubbling air,
circling each other as slowly as fire,
burning with recollections of wedding and proof.
As gods they're not subject to memory's erasure,
and forgiveness is early in its long invention.

Like Penelope searching the face of her husband
Vishnu studies the shifting features of Lakshmi,
her face a land crossed by brilliance and cloud.
Having followed the voice of exquisite illusion,
he faces colours absent from the palette of his prayers,
and sees his true hunted goddess before him.

He finds himself tangled in the fabric of compunction,
and the feathers of peacocks wilt on his lips.

The sting of his insults still cuts her cheek,
blazes like the pouring of butter on fire.
Only gestation makes a woman a goddess –
not the scissoring of one man's mind. But
she can't simply hate him whose breath is her source,
whose thoughts are the ocean on which she floats,
or corrode herself abhorring the sustainer of the Earth.
He is the deer she will hunt for in heaven.

She shamed his name before thousands of creatures,
made him subject to both his body and her.
As he wakes from the blue Rama dream of himself,
he perceives his own piety as an addling of air.
She lent him a heaven he needed to create
when eternity slipped like an eel from his memory.
He takes her as a boy takes the wisdom of his sister
and follows a knowledge he can't yet comprehend.

She sees him, the final blue jewel she still craves.
Even now his blue shoulders form waterfalls in her,
and his eyes mark the birth of her knowledge of love.
He is sweet as the lover who first licked her body,
harsh as the husband who ransacked her dreams.
She swallows the bitter pudding of memory.
She holds him, a universe who didn't know better
bears him as a white horse bears light on its back.

Vishnu and Lakshmi, Rama and Sita
meet in a thin eternal happiness
which neither of their histories will fully allow.

They kiss like memory and old prayers respoken,
the eternal grating of discrepant love.

Lakshmi will return to Earth each year,
and continue to strip herself of all riches.
She'll drop her silk-wrapped packets of prosperity,
dispensing from the sky her mother's abundance.
She'll shed her ornaments to all who receive her,
offering gold like sweet butter to sustain their lives.
And fires for one night will burn only for her reverence.
From heaven she'll plot the renovation of the world,
uphold those who've fallen into sexual disfavour,
and chant the smooth prayers that hold Earth in its orbit.

And Vishnu, like a father wishing a child,
desires to know himself fully enfleshed.
He sees skin is a scripture he can still learn inside of
and imagines a form for his mischief and advancement.
In an eon he'll return as the figure of Krishna,
and know infinite bliss in the castle of his flesh,
in the tresses and shrine of a pure earthly woman.
He'll be swaddled in memorial blue of his skin
and croon with immaculate arpeggios of pleasure,
his fingers dancing flute-like through the staffs of sense.

Notes

Dark One: "Dark One" is one of the epithets of Krishna.

Water-Lilies: These are the large curving paintings by Claude Monet which line the walls of a large basement room in the museum.

Flesh of my Flesh: There is a story that when a human sleeps the god Indra and his partner Indrani are making love inside the sleeping body.

Mount Athos: Mount Athos is a peninsula in Greece which is home to a number of Orthodox monasteries.

Blue Jesus: When still a boy, Krishna defeats the many-headed serpent Kaliya which lives in the Yamuna River.

Radha: Radha is foremost of the devotees of Krishna. She is one of a group of milk-maids (or gopis) who dote on him. She is first in his affections, and the two are often imagined paired in love.

Shiva Nataraja: "Nataraja" means "Lord of the dance." The popular statues of Shiva Nataraja show him with four arms, dancing in a circle of fire, his foot on the child-like figure of ignorance.

Krishna Speaks from the Whirlwind: This poem is a rewriting of the speech which God gives to Job (Job 38-41) as it might be spoken by the Krishna who speaks in *The Bhagavad Gita*.

Avatar: At one point in *The Ramayana*, the gods descend from heaven to remind Rama that he is Vishnu incarnate. Rama, however, seems to forget this revelation. This poem blends thoughts and images of Rama and Jesus as they attempt to slide out of their knowledge of being divine.

Rama and Sita: Sita becomes (or in some versions returns to the form of) the goddess Lakshmi. Lakshmi is the goddess of wealth and prosperity, who is believed to descend to Earth each year on the holiday of Divali to give riches to those who light lamps to greet her.

Acknowledgements

The following books have been helpful in providing stories and ideas for poems:

Ramayana: A Journey by Ranchor Prime (London: Collins & Brown, 1997).

Ramayana by William Buck, illustrated by Shirley Triest (Berkeley and Los Angeles: University of California Press, 1976).

The Ramayana by R.K. Narayan (New York: Penguin, 1977).

Hindu Myths by Wendy Doniger O'Flaherty (London: Penguin, 1975).

The Bhagavad Gita translated by Juan Mascaro (London, Penguin, 1962).

Ka: Stories of the Mind and Gods of India by Roberto Calasso, translated by Tim Parks (New York: Vintage, 1998).

Hinduism and Ecology: Seeds of Truth by Ranchor Prime (London: Cassell, 1992).

Journey Through the Twelve Forests: An Encounter with Krishna by David L. Haberman (New York: Oxford University Press, 1994).

The Sword and the Flute: Kali and Krsna, Dark Visions of the Terrible and the Sublime in Hindu Mythology by David R. Kinsley (Berkeley: University of California Press, 2000).

The Adventures of Young Krishna, the Blue God of India by Diksha Dalal-Clayton, illustrated by Marilyn Heeger (New York: Oxford University Press, 1992).

Tree of Dreams: Ten Tales from the Garden of Night by Lawrence Yep, illustrated by Isadore Seltzer (Mahway, N.J.: BridgeWater Books, 1995).

Some of the poems in this book first appeared in the following publications: *Arc, The Dalhousie Review, Event, Grain, Prairie Fire, Windsor Review,* and *Bent on Writing* (Women's Press, 2002).

This book was produced with the support of the Ontario Arts Council and the City of Toronto through the Toronto Arts Council.

Thanks to Antonio D'Alfonso, Judy Fong Bates, Catherine Graham, Helen Battersby, and Jennifer Morrow for their comments on poems. Thanks also to Janet McClelland, Sutapa Raybardhan, and Bryan Young.

Printed in
November 2004
at Gauvin Press Ltd., Gatineau, Québec